THE
CYPHER FILES

VIKING

an imprint of

PENGUIN BOOKS

HOW TO PLAY

Before you begin, you will need:

- a pencil
- a pair of scissors
- a device connected to the Internet (preferably a smartphone)

As you play through this book, you will encounter two elements:

the puzzle page and the clue page.

STEP 1

Solve the puzzle on the puzzle page.

STEP 2

Visit the URL on the adjacent clue page (you can type the URL in your browser or scan the unique QR code on the page itself).

STEP 3

Submit the answer to the puzzle on screen
(answer correctly and you'll get a clue, usually a word).

STEP 4

Write down the clue (you'll need this for solving
puzzles later in the book).

In the following pages, you'll need to enter these clues
whenever you see a clue box: **[Clue #XX]**.

To solve the puzzles, you'll need to think outside the
book. Write, draw, search, fold and cut pages, explore
virtual escape rooms and think laterally to identify the
perpetrator and solve the mystery.

You don't need a special app to play the game
– any web browser will do.

TURN THE PAGE TO PLAY A DEMO PUZZLE 〉〉〉

0.

CLASSIFIED

Hey! This is just a demo to help you understand how
to play the game.>>>

Check the right page and solve the puzzle >>>

Step 2
*Visit this web address
or scan the QRcode*

↙

Step 3
*Answer correctly
and write down the clue*

↙

CYPHER.CENTER/A/0

[Clue #0]: _____

Scan the QR code or visit the above URL.
Submit the answer and collect the page clue.

Step 1
This is the puzzle page.
Solve this:

30+12

ABOUT CY.P.H.E.R.

In this book, you are an agent of CY.P.H.E.R.

CY.P.H.E.R. (CYphers, Puzzles, Heiroglyphs and Enigmas Reconaissance) is an international agency tasked to investigate any case national security agencies consider impossible to solve.

The agency performs complex investigations using cutting edge digital codebreaking technology along with old-fashioned analogue techniques.

The men and women of CY.P.H.E.R. are ordinary people who do extraordinary things. They have a very strong ethos of public service, and yet their work often goes unnoticed in the public domain.

They are tirelessly professional and ethical in the way they conduct their work and their high ideals are reflected in their cryptonyms, as all agents are given eponymous handles based on the Knights of the Round Table.

The Director General is known only as 'Arthur'.

File: #AL1A5

CLASSIFIED

We have been assigned a case by THE ORG.

Three people have been reported missing during the last nine days
in the city of Norton. All three individuals appear to be unrelated
and no discernible link exists between the three cases.

Given that there hasn't been a missing persons case in Norton for
decades, we need to assess if these cases are in any way connected.

Galahad is assigned as field agent, conducting all necessary in
situ research, while Bedivere will provide tech support and cyber
intelligence from HQ.

For security reasons, Galahad will report officially to Bedivere,
and Bedivere will relay the reports to Arthur on a daily basis. No
action is to be taken unless previously authorised by HQ.

Arthur//

CLASSIFIED

A402 is a photographer.

She was reported missing by her roommate 9 days ago.

According to her roommate, one day prior to her disappearance, she came home after a nature photography session and was acting strangely, reciting seemingly random numbers and then writing them down on pieces of paper.

Between these incidents she had no recollection of her acting in this way and couldn't explain the significance of the numbers. The next day she left the apartment at 10am.

At 11am her roommate received a text message with a string of numbers. A402 has not been seen or heard of since.

Bedivere//

CYPHER.CENTER/A/01

[Clue #01]:

Scan the QR code or visit the above URL.
Submit the answer and collect the page clue.

MP.ID: A402

Name: Lena █████████
Gender: Female
Height: 169 cm
Weight: 54 kg
Eye Color: Brown
Hair Color: Brown
Occupation: Photographer

A402's roommate received the following text message in the wake of her disappearance:

"63.446110 10.898954"

What is this?

CLASSIFIED

We have collected recent fingerprints from A402's camera. We need to crosscheck them with an older fingerprint we have on file in our database archive.

Bedivere//

CYPHER.CENTER/A/02

[Clue #02]:

Scan the QR code or visit the above URL.
Submit the answer and collect the page clue.

FINGERPRINTS COMPARISON
SUBJECT ID: A402

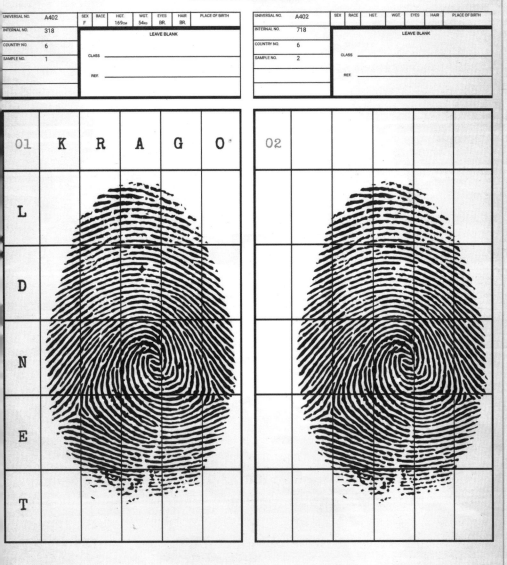

UNIVERSAL NO.	A402
INTERNAL NO.	318
COUNTRY NO.	6
SAMPLE NO.	1

SEX	RACE	HGT.	WGT.	EYES	HAIR	PLACE OF BIRTH
F		169CM	54KG	BR.	BR.	

LEAVE BLANK

CLASS _____

REF. _____

UNIVERSAL NO.	A402
INTERNAL NO.	718
COUNTRY NO.	6
SAMPLE NO.	2

SEX	RACE	HGT.	WGT.	EYES	HAIR	PLACE OF BIRTH

LEAVE BLANK

CLASS _____

REF. _____

01 K R A G O

02

L

D

N

E

T

CLASSIFIED

A403 teaches maths at Norton High School.

He has been missing for 6 days.

His students report that he was extremely absent-minded in class the day before he disappeared.

Nothing the students did bothered him or made him react in any way. The last thing he did before he left the class was to fill the entire blackboard with nonsensical numbers and words.

He has not be seen since.

Bedivere//

CYPHER.CENTER/A/03

[Clue #03]: ‎

Scan the QR code or visit the above URL.
Submit the answer and collect the page clue.

MP.ID: A403

Name: John ▮▮▮▮▮
Gender: Male
Height: 180 cm
Weight: 83 kg
Eye Color: Brown
Hair Color: Brown
Occupation: Mathematician

a blackboard found in the missing person's apartment. It seems that is the last thing he wrote

CLASSIFIED

We have provided you with A403's fingerprints from our database archive.

Collect a recent fingerprint from the classroom and carry out a cross-examination.

Bedivere//

CYPHER.CENTER/A/04

[Clue #04]: _____

Scan the QR code or visit the above URL.
Submit the answer and collect the page clue.

FINGERPRINTS ANALYSIS
SUBJECT ID: A403

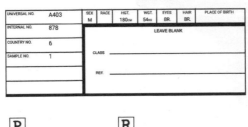

UNIVERSAL NO.	A403	SEX	RACE	HGT.	WGT.	EYES	HAIR	PLACE OF BIRTH
		M		180cm	54kg	BR.	BR.	
INTERNAL NO.	878							
COUNTRY NO.	6			LEAVE BLANK				
SAMPLE NO.	1	CLASS _____						
		REF. _____						

CLASSIFIED

A405 is a research chemist, developing a new form of electric arc furnace for the local cast iron foundry.

His colleagues report that the day before he disappeared, he had several panic attacks during which he was nervous and agitated to the point of being aggressive. Each of these episodes lasted for 5 to 10 minutes and they posed great danger to everyone in the lab, as the argon gas used for shielding the iron cast reaction was left unsupervised and there was a serious danger of leakage.

All A405's colleagues say that this was highly unlike him.
They describe him as a very mild and calm person, sometimes even making fun of him for his zen-like attitude.

Some of them had apparently called him a 'tree-hugger' behind his back, after reportedly seeing him actually doing that on his frequent nature walks...

Bedivere//

CYPHER.CENTER/A/05

[Clue #05]:

Scan the QR code or visit the above URL.
Submit the answer and collect the page clue.

MP.ID: A405

Name: Jason ▮▮▮▮
Gender: Male
Height: 172 cm
Weight: 69 kg
Eye Color: Green
Hair Color: Brown
Occupation: Chemist

*a table full
of iron and argon*

CFID:DE

CLASSIFIED

We have provided you with a recent fingerprint from the lab and one from our database archive, for cross-examination.

Bedivere//

CYPHER.CENTER/A/06

[Clue #06]: ████████████

Scan the QR code or visit the above URL.
Submit the answer and collect the page clue.

FINGERPRINTS CONNECTIONS
SUBJECT ID: A405

UNIVERSAL NO.	A405	SEX	RACE	HGT.	WGT.	EYES	HAIR	PLACE OF BIRTH
		M		172CM	69KG	GR.	BR.	
INTERNAL NO.	7844				LEAVE BLANK			
COUNTRY NO.	6							
SAMPLE NO.	4	CLASS						
		REF.						

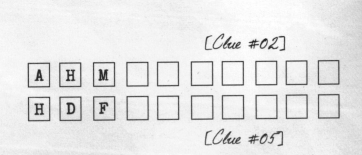

A	A	S	R
E	H	M	L
D	D	F	N

[Clue #02]

A	H	M						
H	D	F						

[Clue #05]

CLASSIFIED

You have been asked to send in your report regarding the Norton missing persons case no later than 5pm today.

Be brief and precise.

Bedivere//

It's a good thing I started working on it last night. I just need to fill in their data and I'm done.

CYPHER.CENTER/A/07

[Clue #07]:

Scan the QR code or visit the above URL.
Submit the answer and collect the page clue.

CY.P.H.E.R.
DO NOT COPY/CONFIDENTIAL
FILE: #AL1A5

MP.ID: *A403*

Surname: |_|_|_|_|_|_|_|_|_|_|

[Clue #01]

MP.ID: *A402*

Surname: |_|_|_|_|_|_|_|_|_|_|

[Clue #04]

MP.ID: *A405*

Surname: |_|_|_|_|_|_|_|_|_|_|

[Clue #06]

MP.ID:

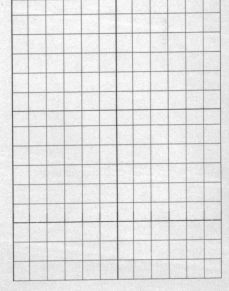

Surname: |_|_|_|_|_|_|_|_|_|_|

CLASSIFIED

This is what we received from THE ORG today.
Read it and act accordingly:

"With regards to your official report regarding the Norton missing persons case, we authorise you to proceed with your investigation. We have full confidence in your ability to analyze the data that has been collected thus far, and deduct the location and identity of the next victim. THE ORG"

Bedivere//

CYPHER.CENTER/A/08

[Clue #08]:

Scan the QR code or visit the above URL.
Submit the answer and collect the page clue.

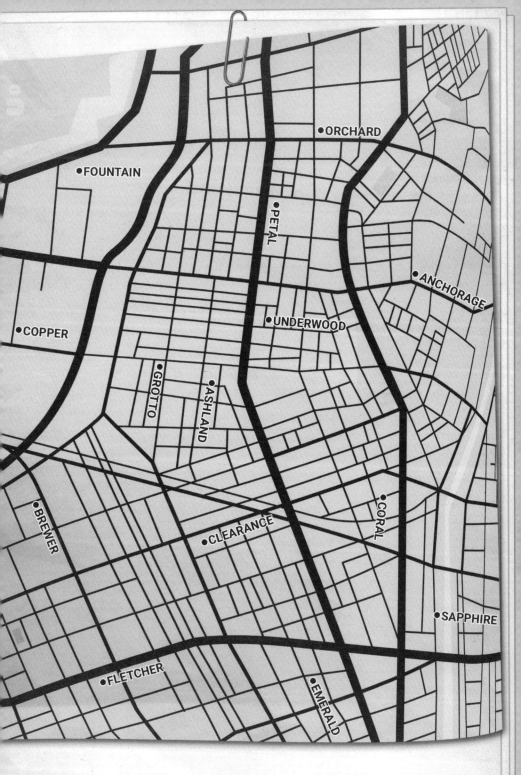

[Clue #02] Fletcher [Clue #03]
Brewer [Clue #05] [Clue #02]

09

CLASSIFIED

Following your investigation results, we have compiled a list of possible future victims living in the designated location.

Use this list to locate who the next victim will be and notify CY.P.H.E.R. immediately.

Do not —repeat – do not – take action yourself once you locate the next victim.

Bedivere//

CYPHER.CENTER/A/09

[Clue #09]:

Scan the QR code or visit the above URL.
Submit the answer and collect the page clue.

A	L	B	E	R	T	L
N	W	L	E	N	N	U
D	T	I	M	A	Y	T
E	U	J	L	R	R	H
R	R	A	A	S	A	E
S	N	M	A	T	O	R
O	E	E	L	I	V	N
N	R	S	H	A	R	A

POSSIBLE NEXT VICTIMS:

ALBERT LUTHER
JAMES ANDERSON
MAY TURNER
MAT LENN
SHARA BEAR
NYRA LIV
MARY ███████

who is next?

CFID:MA

10

File: #AL1A5

CLASSIFIED

A8199 did not show up for work today and is not at home.

It is too soon for A8199 to be characterised as a missing person, but we must act as if this is the case if we are to solve this. Locate and secure A8199.

Bedivere//

CYPHER.CENTER/A/10

[Clue #10]:

Scan the QR code or visit the above URL.
Submit the answer and collect the page clue.

MP.ID: A8199

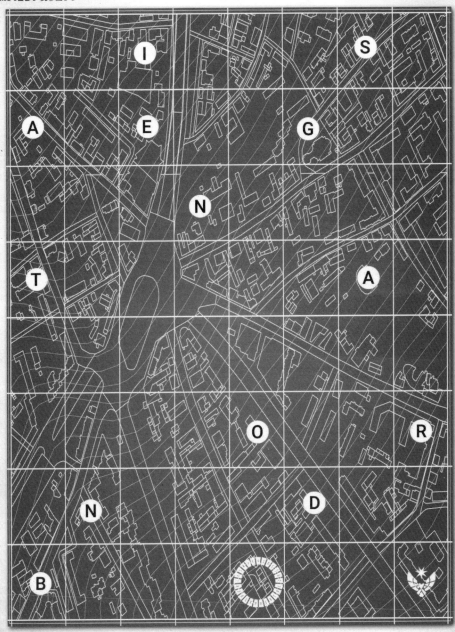

I am a [Clue #07] until the N
then I am a [Clue #09]

11

CLASSIFIED

A8199 has been hospitalised and placed under police custody, suffering from severe detachment and psychotic behaviour.

THE ORG is rather hostile and won't share any information with us whatsoever. If we are to get to the bottom of this case, we need to find a way to read the medical record.

Bedivere//

CYPHER.CENTER/A/11

[Clue #11]: ⬛⬛⬛⬛⬛⬛⬛⬛⬛⬛

Scan the QR code or visit the above URL.
Submit the answer and collect the page clue.

CY.P.H.E.R.
DO NOT COPY/CONFIDENTIAL
FILE: #AL1A5

Hospital Address: CYPHER.CENTER/ [Clue #10]

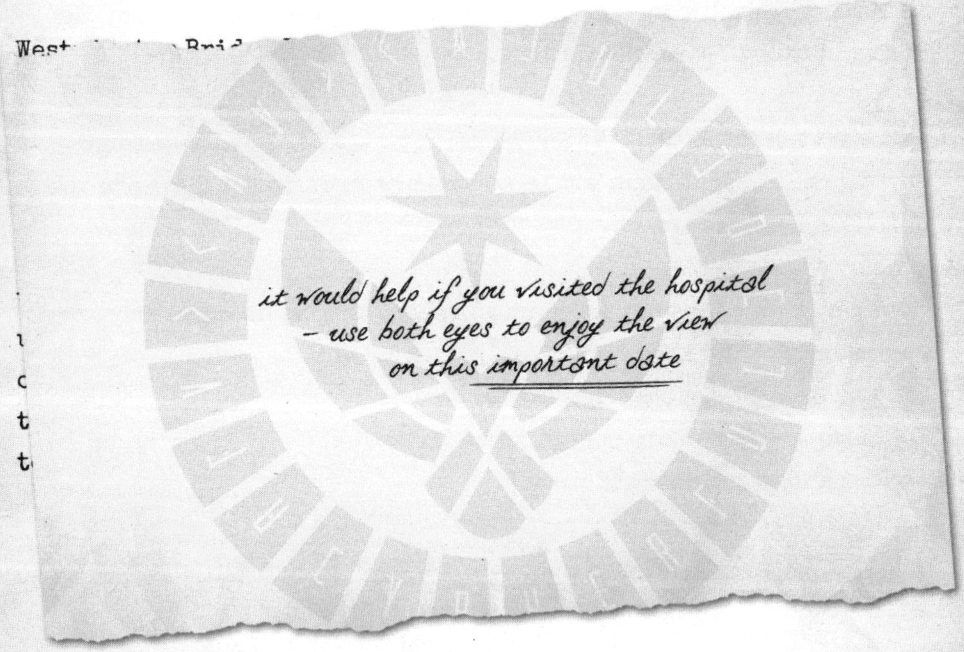

it would help if you visited the hospital
- use both eyes to enjoy the view
on this important date

CFID:NA

File: #AL1A5

CLASSIFIED

It is highly probable that THE ORG will officially take over this case and take CY.P.H.E.R. off it.

We need to get THE ORG's internal report regarding A8199 and go through their findings, while we still have official access to the case files.

However, since they expected us to snoop, they've changed passwords to hinder us until they officially kick us out.

You need to get us this report so we know what's really going on in Norton and why they want us out.

Bedivere//

CYPHER.CENTER/A/12

[Clue #12]:

Scan the QR code or visit the above URL.
Submit the answer and collect the page clue.

CY.P.H.E.R.
DO NOT COPY/CONFIDENTIAL
FILE: #AL1A5

"After the Chernobyl incident, nobody in Egypt plays arcade games anymore."

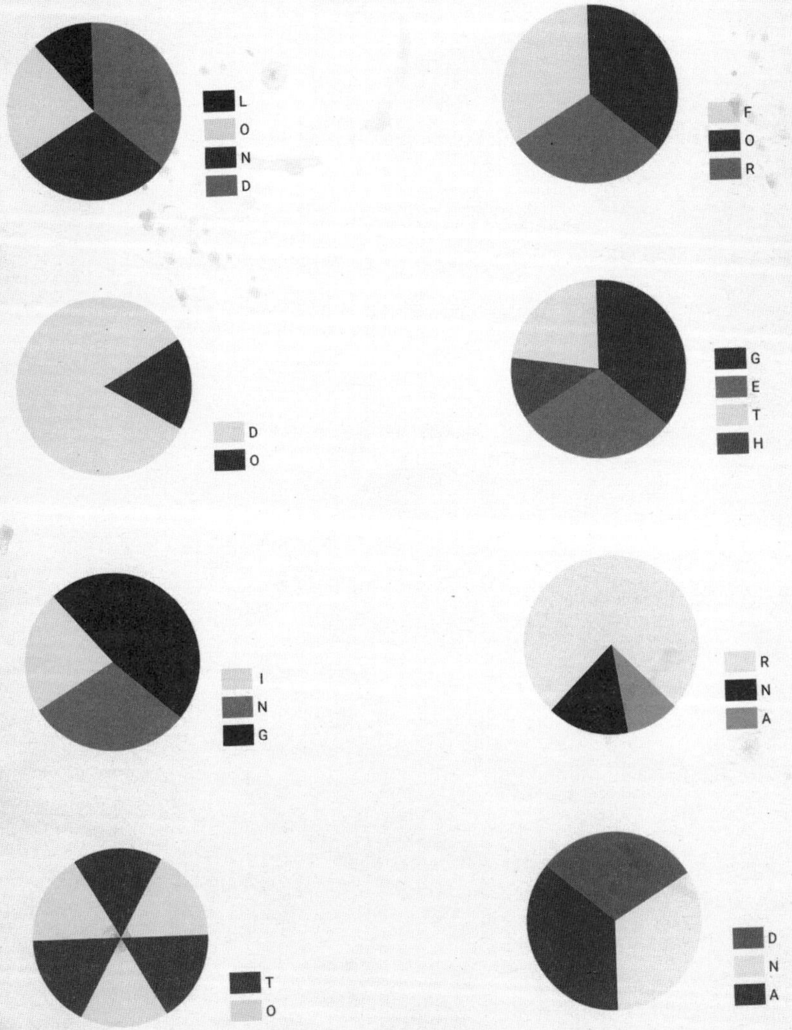
L
O
N
D
F
O
R
D
O
G
E
T
H
I
N
G
R
N
A
T
O
D
N
A

CFID:KR

13.

CLASSIFIED

We have officially been asked to close the Norton case and hand over all our research.

Upload everything you've got to the database before coming back to HQ to report in person.

Bedivere//

*It's not over yet!
If I show Bedivere the
redacted paragraph,
we will have a chance
to stay on the case.*

CYPHER.CENTER/A/13

[Clue #13]:

Scan the QR code or visit the above URL.
Submit the answer and collect the page clue.

```
def process_request(request, user, password, failed_aftertry):
    """
    This method will proceed the request
    Args:
        request:
        user:
        org_password.rebus
        failed_aftertry:
    Returns:
    """
-------------------------------------------------------------------"
                result += "\n[+] THEORG \nCredentials succeed to
Log:\n> username: " + user + " and " \
"password: " \
"" + password
                result += "\n[+]
--------------------------------------*-----------------------------\n
"
                with open("./results.cyp", "w+") as frr:
                    frr.write(result)
                print(
                    "[+] A Match succeed 'user: " + user + " and
password: " + password + "' and have been saved at "
"./results.cyp")
                exit()
    _token = ""
    try:
        _token = list(set(tree.xpath("//input[@name='" +
csrf_field + "']/@value")))[0]
    except Exception as es: pass
return _token
-----------------------------------------------------------------
  org_password:
```

```
"                                                                    "
"                                                                    "
"                \     /                                             "
"            \    # ^ #    /                                         "
"             \  (     ) /                                           "
"     _____(%%%%%%%)_____                              "
"    (    /  / )%%%%%%%( \  \    )                                   "
"    (__/___/__/          _____) +4     2+[Clue #11]            "
"      (    / /(%%%%%%%)\ \   )                                      "
"      (__/___/ (%%%%%%) \___\__)                                    "
"             /(      )\                                             "
"            /   (%%%%%)   \           I think I know                "
"               (%%%)                  the org-password...           "
"                 !                                                  "
"                                                                    "
"                                                                    "
-----------------------------------------------------------------
CFID:RI
```

CLASSIFIED

THE ORG has informed us that you haven't uploaded your research to the database.

We are no longer on this case, so any further hesitation from your part will have disciplinary consequences.

Hand over your research and report back to HQ ASAP.

Bedivere//

CYPHER.CENTER/A/14

[Clue #14]:

Scan the QR code or visit the above URL.
Submit the answer and collect the page clue.

Communicate with all departments and agents ONLY through
the secure line: CYPHER.CENTER/ [Clue #13]

Agent ID.:	#Number:
M.P.	97312
E.P.	93766
D.C.	95834
I.M.	92674
GD Arthur	9xxxx

I need to call the boss personally.
If I get him on the phone, he will listen...

15

CLASSIFIED

THE ORG has a new case that seems to fit the pattern.
They codenamed the victim M7016 – he works as a librarian in
Norton High School.

He seems to have gone missing the moment A8199 was put under
police custody.

THE ORG has already put together a team working to locate M7016,
but more importantly, they are putting together another team to
"find a solution from the past before this escalates even further".

I don't know what this means, but we have to work it out quickly.
First, let's find out who M7016 is.

Bedivere//

CYPHER.CENTER/A/15

[Clue #15]:

Scan the QR code or visit the above URL.
Submit the answer and collect the page clue.

Literature [Clue #08]

16

CLASSIFIED

All missing persons except M7016 left hidden clues right before they disappeared.

If his disappearance is linked to the others, he must have left something too.

Search his apartment and see what you can find.

Bedivere//

CYPHER.CENTER/A/16

[Clue #16]: _____

Scan the QR code or visit the above URL.
Submit the answer and collect the page clue.

Apartment Address: CYPHER.CENTER/ [Clue #12]

135
215
45
360
0

17

File: #AL1A5

CLASSIFIED

Arthur is expecting an in-person briefing from you and has denied receiving any briefing from me.

You either come here and follow disciplinary action, or find a way to get him on the phone, explain yourself and convince him to get you off the hook.

Bedivere//

CYPHER.CENTER/A/17

[Clue #17]:

Scan the QR code or visit the above URL.
Submit the answer and collect the page clue.

CY.P.H.E.R.
DO NOT COPY/CONFID3NTIAL
FILE: #AL1A5

Communicate with all departments and agents ONLY through the secure line.
The address of the secure line is the same, but Arthur's number has changed.
His last known number will help you to find his new one.

	8	9	7
16[Clue #16] >			
[Clue #14]-[Clue #15] >			
	*	0	#

CFID:ON

CLASSIFIED

What we have in our hands is not enough to make our case and obtain the access we need. I propose we take it to the streets.

Ask around and see if there are any elderly locals who can remember any strange incidents from their childhood, either first-hand or as a rumour.

Bedivere//

CYPHER.CENTER/A/18

[Clue #18］:

Scan the QR code or visit the above URL.
Submit the answer and collect the page clue.

POI.ID: W302

Name: Jim McAvoy
Gender: Male
DOB: 12/11/1931

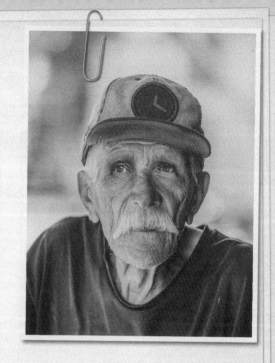

LOG ENTRY #	TIME STAMP	
1	12:00:30	
2	11:03:55	
3	01:21:15	
4	03:00:00	
		It was about time to find
		someone who can help...
		Log entries:
		4, 1, 2, 3, 3, 2, 1, 4

CFID:OZ

19.

CLASSIFIED

I went over your report and he seems very promising.
See what you can find out by interviewing him and fill me in.

Bedivere//

CYPHER.CENTER/A/19

[Clue #19]:

Scan the QR code or visit the above URL.
Submit the answer and collect the page clue.

He has something to show me.
We'll meet at the exit...

Start from (A) >>>

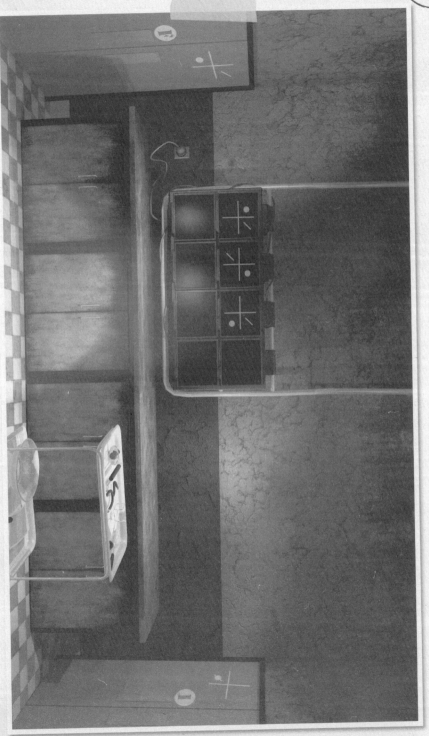

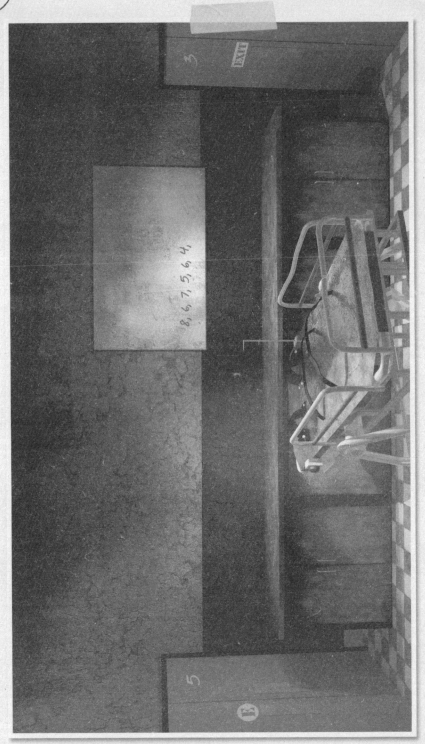

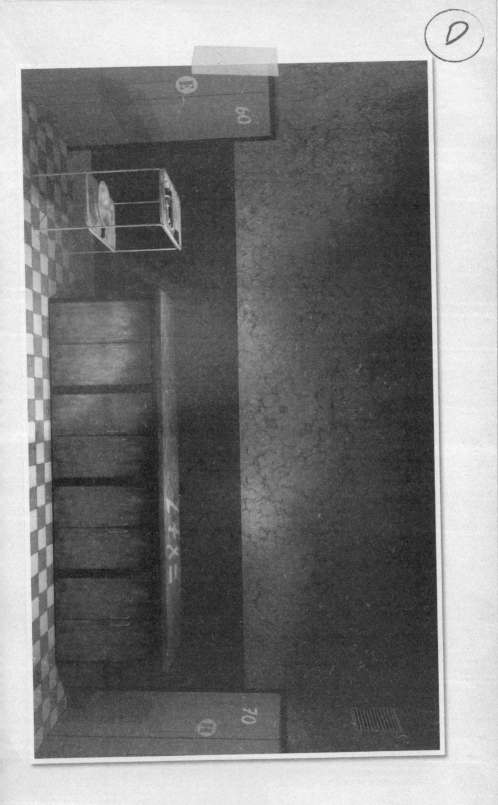

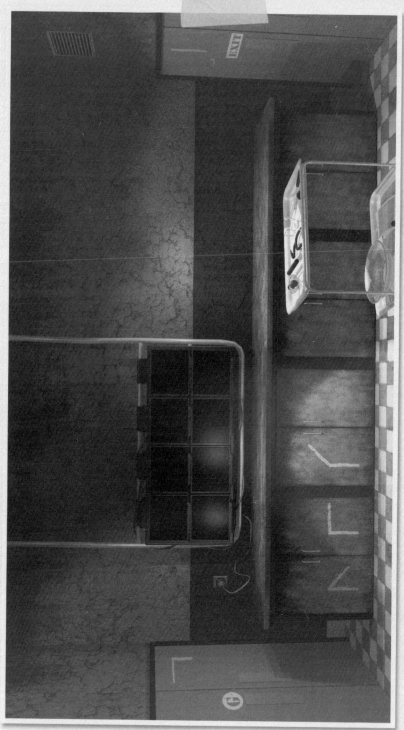

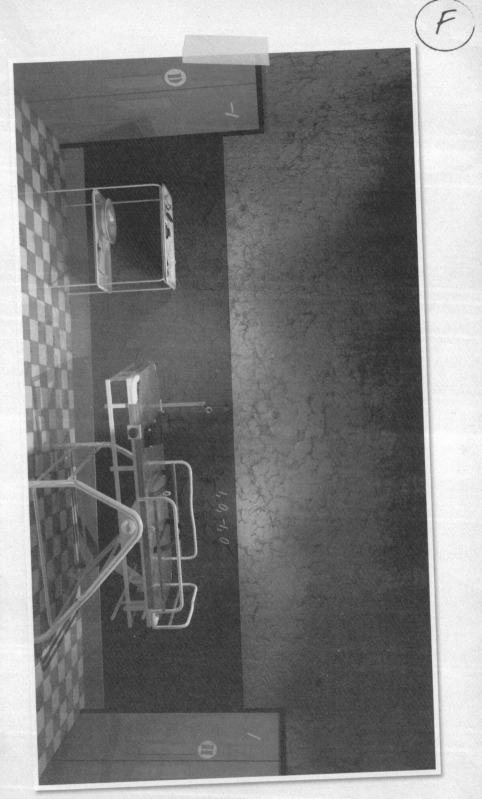

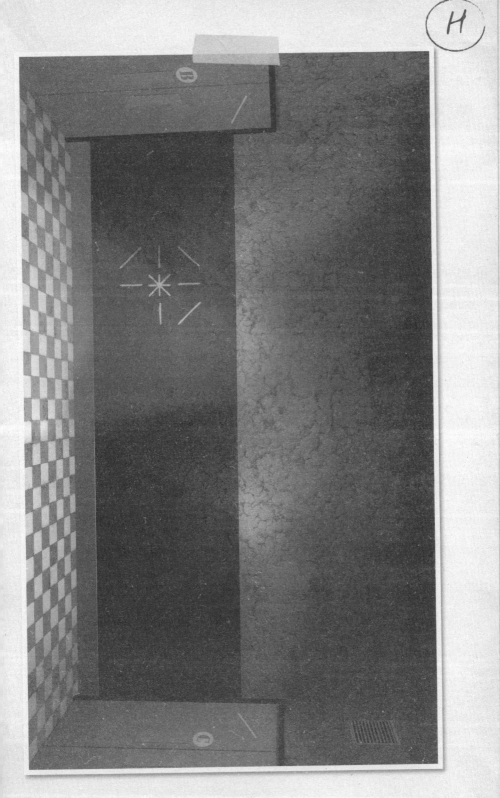

1

What's the word he needs to hear?

File: #AL1A5

CLASSIFIED

I cannot find anything that confirms what you told me.
Furthermore, I tried to hack into the archives and it's impossible.

The only thing we can do now is for you to dig deeper into what the
old man knows and gather as much information about the incident as
possible.

Then, we engage Arthur for the last time.

So we'd better build a rock-solid case as soon as possible.

Bedivere//

CYPHER.CENTER/A/20

[Clue #20]:

Scan the QR code or visit the above URL.
Submit the answer and collect the page clue.

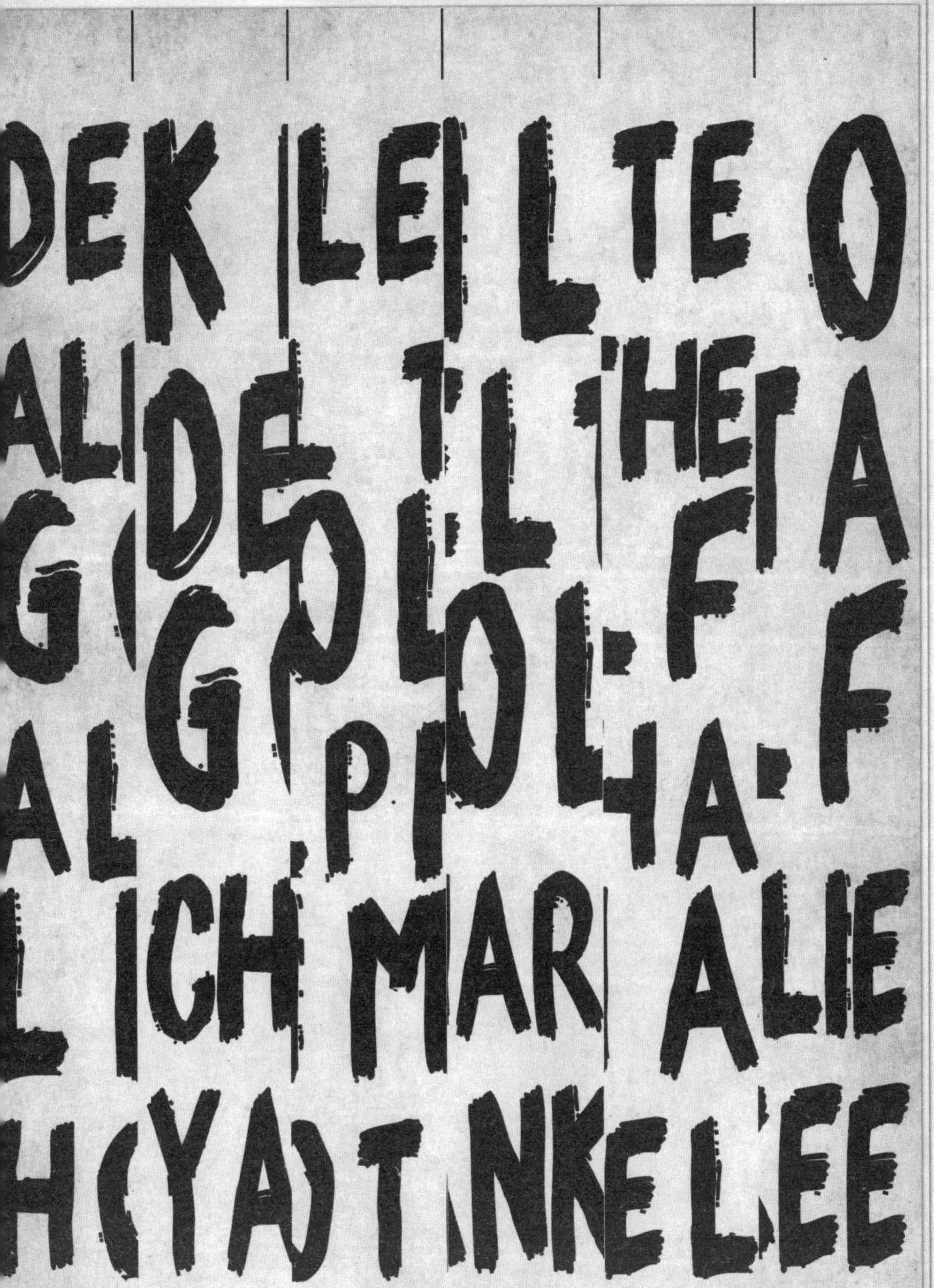

DEK |LE| L TE O

AL DE T |HE|

G |DE| L L F A

AL G DL F

AL G PP L4· F

L ICH MAR ALIE

H(YA) T NKE LEE

ANLGEDHUKCGRYO

+[Clue #18]

I found these in the lab.
The documents are connected somehow

21

CLASSIFIED

I found a local newspaper that describes the missing persons case in Norton back in 1942.

This verifies the old man's story, to some extent. Someone – or some organisation – has done their best to erase this from history.

Dive deeper into the case and I'll see what more I can dig up.

And sorry for yesterday. You have to admit you would have had trouble believing me if I told you this, right?

Bedivere//

CYPHER.CENTER/A/21

[Clue #21]: _____

Scan the QR code or visit the above URL.
Submit the answer and collect the page clue.

SCIENCE AND MEDICINE

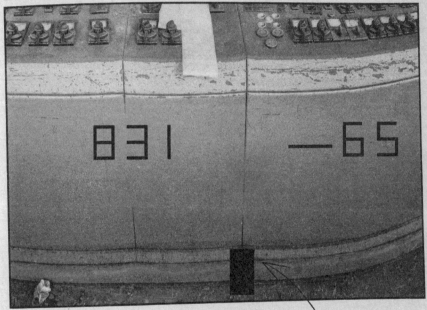

The alias experiment control room

[Clue #17] [Clue #20]

22

File: #AL1A5

CLASSIFIED

The intel you gathered is very valuable, but we need one more detail in order to be able to present our case to Arthur and get his support.

Find out how the old man's story ended, so we can not only present the case to Arthur, but also have a plan of action ready to go.

To show up with a strange story and no plan of action would be a bad move...

Bedivere//

CYPHER.CENTER/A/22

[Clue #22]: _____

Scan the QR code or visit the above URL.
Submit the answer and collect the page clue.

161245? [Clue #11]

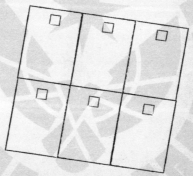

I have a copy of these pages at the end of the folder

23.

CLASSIFIED

It's time to engage Arthur for the last time.

Regrettably, after our last attempt to speak to him, he burned both his phone and his Signal account.

Find a way to get through to him and once you do, let me do the talking this time.

Bedivere//

CYPHER.CENTER/A/23

[Clue #23]: ▐▬▬▬▬▬▬▬▬▬▬▬▬▬▌

Scan the QR code or visit the above URL.
Submit the answer and collect the page clue.

Perhaps I can find some spare parts
at the warehouse to fix this old device

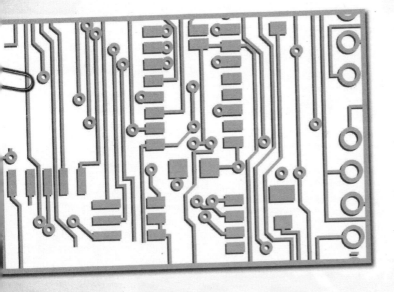

Outline
and multiply by [Clue #21] >>>

52

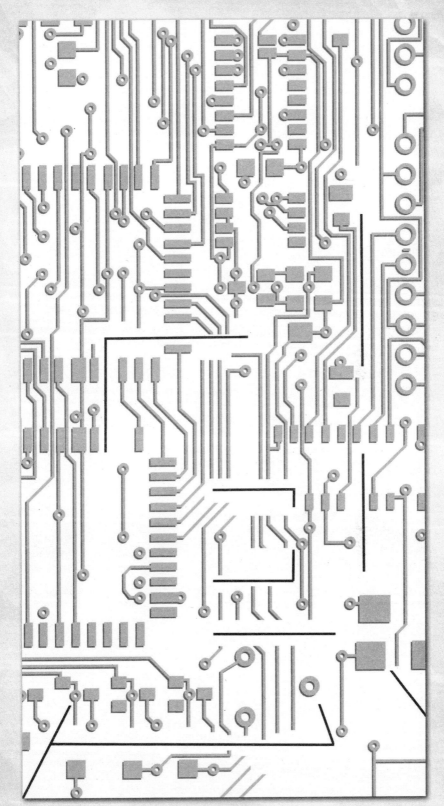

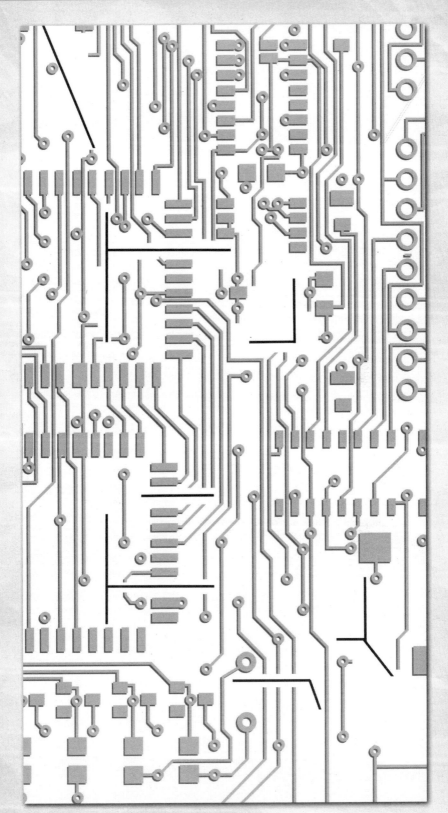

73

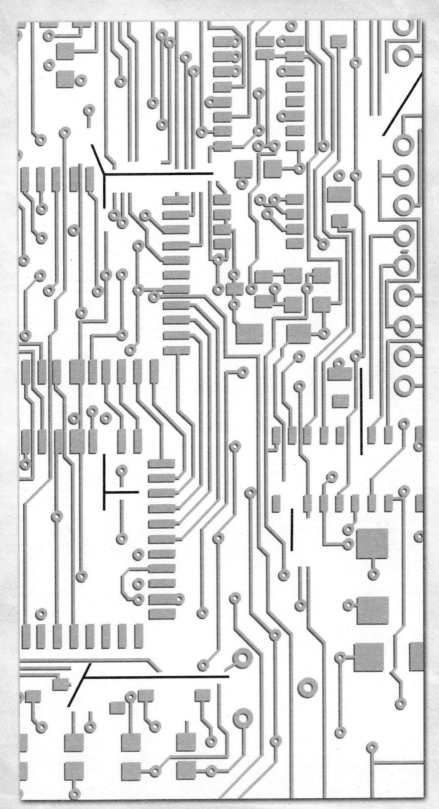

29

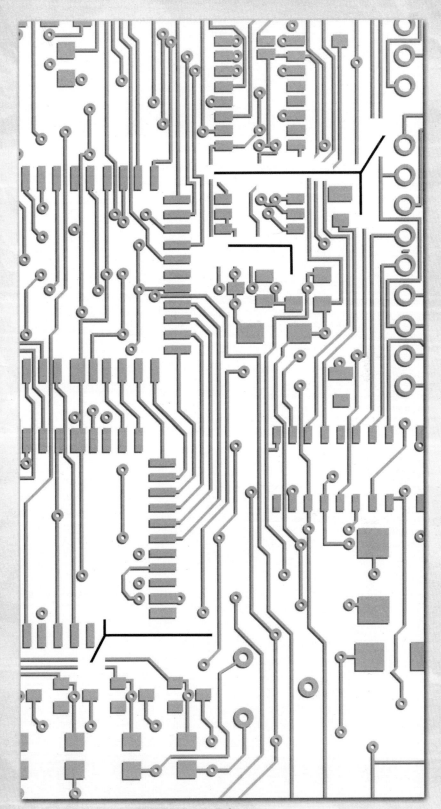

24

CLASSIFIED

Using high clearance from CY.P.H.E.R., we are able to access the archives that were out of reach.

However, it's not that straighforward, as these archives are a constant struggle to navigate due to their high security protocols.

Using the codes I sent you, dive in and get us something we can use in order to solve the case.

Bedivere//

CYPHER.CENTER/A/24

[Clue #24]:

Scan the QR code or visit the above URL.
Submit the answer and collect the page clue.

CY.P.H.E.R.
DO NOT COPY/CON5IDENTIAL*
FILE: #AL1A5

* Never realised this before

*CFID:TE

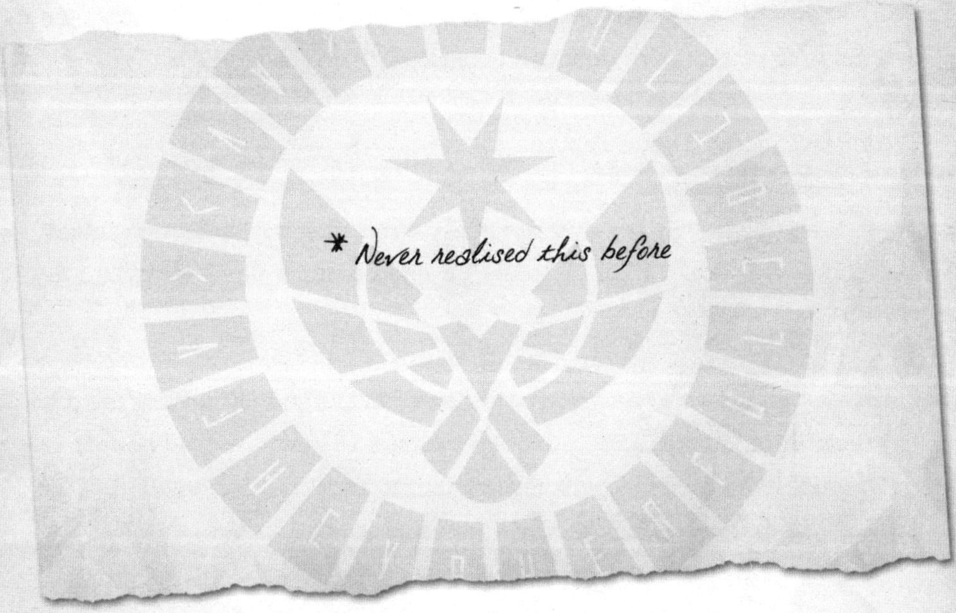

25

File: #AL1A5

CLASSIFIED

If I read this from any other person, in any other circumstance, I would have dismissed it as a wacky conspiracy theory in less than a second and would have ordered a full psychiatric evaluation.

That was too much even for me.

I wonder if this can get any weirder, but since we haven't reached the end yet, I bet it will. I think we need to find the location in which the incident took place.

I won't comment on what you found, as I still find this very hard to believe. Continue digging deeper and see if you can find something we can use. And something to convince me as well, because I feel I'm losing you here.

Bedivere//

CYPHER.CENTER/A/25

[Clue #25]: ▭

Scan the QR code or visit the above URL.
Submit the answer and collect the page clue.

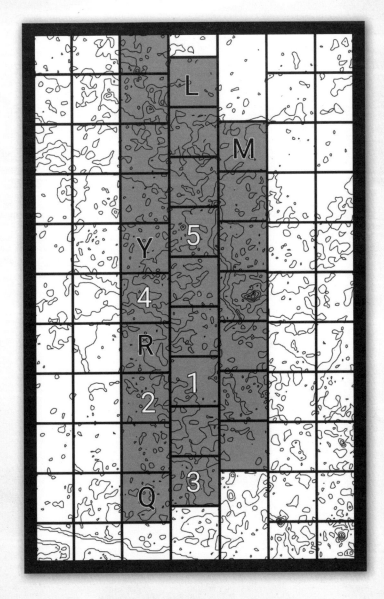

1, 2, 3, 4, 5
+
[Clue #24]

26

CLASSIFIED

The missing persons have been located exactly where you said they would be. The bad news is that it is not safe to just show up and rescue them because we don't know where the perpetrator is, as he hasn't been located by the high altitude drones scanning the area.

This means we must be extra careful and locate who and where the perpetrator is, before moving in to liberate the hostages.

Use the scan report to figure out where the perpetrator is hiding and report back.

Do not – REPEAT – do not take action.

Bedivere//

CYPHER.CENTER/A/26

[Clue #26]: _____

Scan the QR code or visit the above URL.
Submit the answer and collect the page clue.

CY.P.H.E.R.
DO NOT COPY/CONFIDENTIAL
FILE: #AL1A5

Area Scan Report

Priority: Top
Detail: High

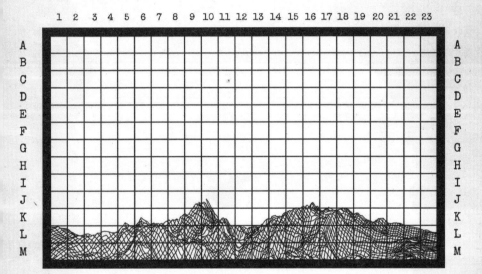

Results:

C10 C11 C12 D12 E12 F12 G12 G11 G10 E10 E11

[Clue #25]

C17 D17 E17 F17 G17 E18 C19 D19 E19 F19 G19

CFID:VI

27

CLASSIFIED

Due to the incriminating allegations that have been circulating in the press since yesterday, CY.P.H.E.R. suspends your function as an agent.

You must immediately return to HQ for a full internal investigation regarding your actions.

Failure to comply with these orders will result in immediate imprisonment and trial with charges of high treason.

CY.P.H.E.R.
The Director General

Arthur

*The Org got to me.
I must play my last card before
it's too late for me and everyone else...*

CYPHER.CENTER/A/27

[Clue #27]: _____

Scan the QR code or visit the above URL.
Submit the answer and collect the page clue.

CY.P.H.E.R.
DO NOT COPY/CONFIDENTIAL
FILE: #AL1A5

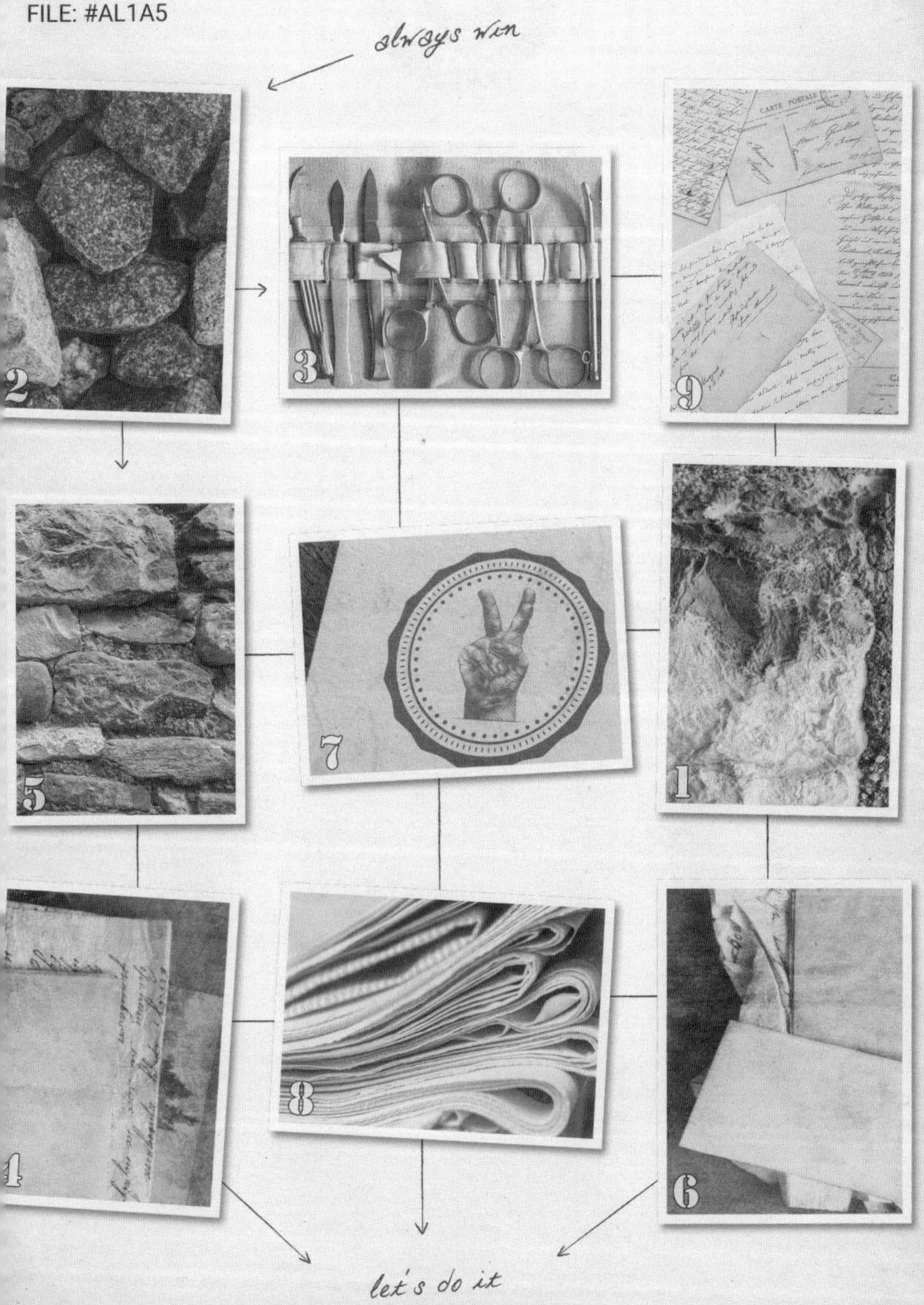
always win
2
3
9
5
7
1
4
8
6
let's do it

CFID:HE

CLASSIFIED

I'd better be fast in finding a way to kill it before they find me and lock me up.
But how could I do it without hurting the hostages?!

CY.P.H.E.R.
DO NOT COPY/CONFIDENTIAL
FILE: #AL1A5

Location: CYPHER.CENTER/ [Clue #27][Clue #26]

[Clue #12] >						
[Clue #19] >						
[Clue #22] >						
[Clue #23] >						
T	H	E	☆	E	N	D

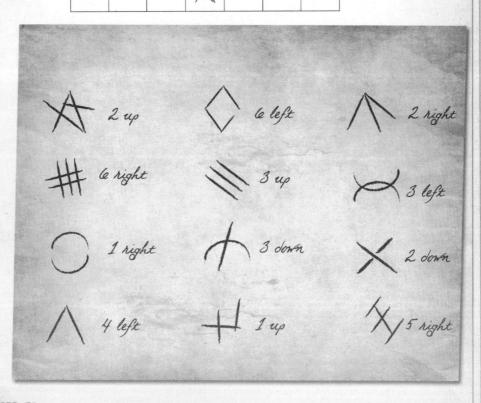

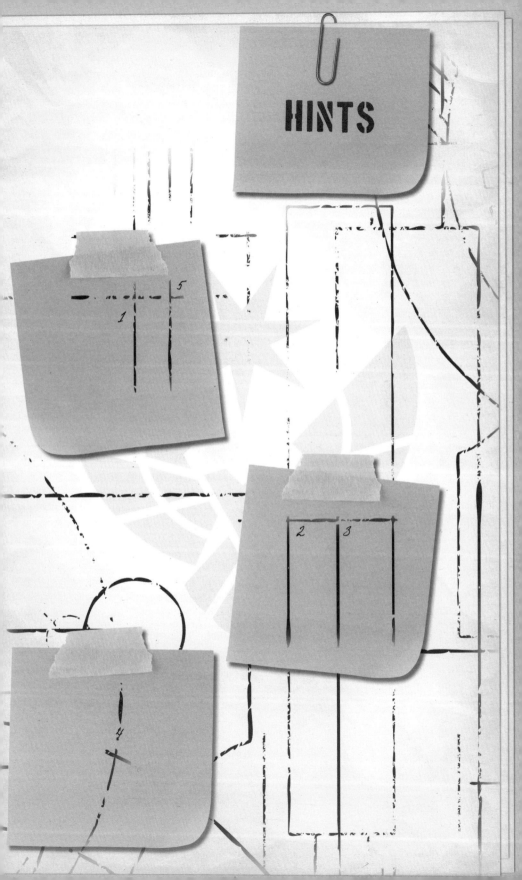

CLASSIFIED

HINT 01.

HINT 01//
I hear Trøndelag in Norway is lovely at this time of year – though you'll need a map.

HINT 02.

HINT 02//
Spot the difference!

CYPHER.CENTER/A/HINTS

For more hints, scan the QR code or visit the above URL.

HINT 03.

HINT 03//
This puzzle is hellish but the solution is the opposite.

HINT 04.

HINT 04//
The solution to this puzzle will a-maze you.

CYPHER.CENTER/A/HINTS

For more hints, scan the QR code or visit the above URL.

HINT 05.

HINT 05//
The table may be of periodic interest.

HINT 06.

HINT 06//
What connects the letters?

CYPHER.CENTER/A/HINTS

For more hints, scan the QR code or visit the above URL.

HINT 07.

HINT 07//
Nice shirt!

HINT 08.

HINT 08//
You might need to get your pencil out for this one –
it's astronomical ...

CYPHER.CENTER/A/HINTS

For more hints, scan the QR code or visit the above URL.

HINT 09.

HINT 09//
You're going to need to do some redacting.

HINT 10.

HINT 10//
Checkmate.

CYPHER.CENTER/A/HINTS

For more hints, scan the QR code or visit the above URL.

HINT 11.

HINT 11//
Those numbers are giving me a sinking feeling ...

HINT 12.

HINT 12//
This one's easy as pie – if you know your hazard symbols,
video games and Egyptian history.

CYPHER.CENTER/A/HINTS

For more hints, scan the QR code or visit the above URL.

HINT 13.

HINT 13//
Doesn't matter what day it is, if you've ever solved a rebus you can get this one.

HINT 14.

HINT 14//
This puzzle is pretty black and white – but you'll need to phone all your friends.

CYPHER.CENTER/A/HINTS

For more hints, scan the QR code or visit the above URL.

HINT 15.

HINT 15//
If you're a librarian, you will have got this one quickly –
otherwise the first letters of the book titles might give
you a clue.

HINT 16.

HINT 16//
You'll work this one out once you've found North.

CYPHER.CENTER/A/HINTS

For more hints, scan the QR code or visit the above URL.

HINT 17.

HINT 17//
Pick up your phone and try to remember your high school
maths lessons.

HINT 18.

HINT 18//
Hats off to Jim for helping with this one.

CYPHER.CENTER/A/HINTS

For more hints, scan the QR code or visit the above URL.

HINT 19.

HINT 19//
Make sure you go through the right doors.

HINT 20.

HINT 20//
Time to get the old squeezebox out.

CYPHER.CENTER/A/HINTS

For more hints, scan the QR code or visit the above URL.

HINT 21.

HINT 21//
If you've solved this puzzle, you may have a small rectangle
of ink on the end of your nose.

HINT 22.

HINT 22//
The cards will reveal the day.

CYPHER.CENTER/A/HINTS

For more hints, scan the QR code or visit the above URL.

HINT 23.

HINT 23//
Once the lines are all on the same page, the door
will be revealed.

HINT 24.

HINT 24//
You're going to need to go back to the beginning to
solve this one.

CYPHER.CENTER/A/HINTS

For more hints, scan the QR code or visit the above URL.

HINT 25.

HINT 25//
Flip the grid 90 degrees clockwise, if that's your
type of thing.

HINT 26.

HINT 26//
Time to go back to art school.

CYPHER.CENTER/A/HINTS

For more hints, scan the QR code or visit the above URL.

CLASSIFIED

HINT 27.

HINT 27//
You have to win every time to get this one.

HINT 28.

HINT 28//
It's all symbolical.

CYPHER.CENTER/A/HINTS

For more hints, scan the QR code or visit the above URL.

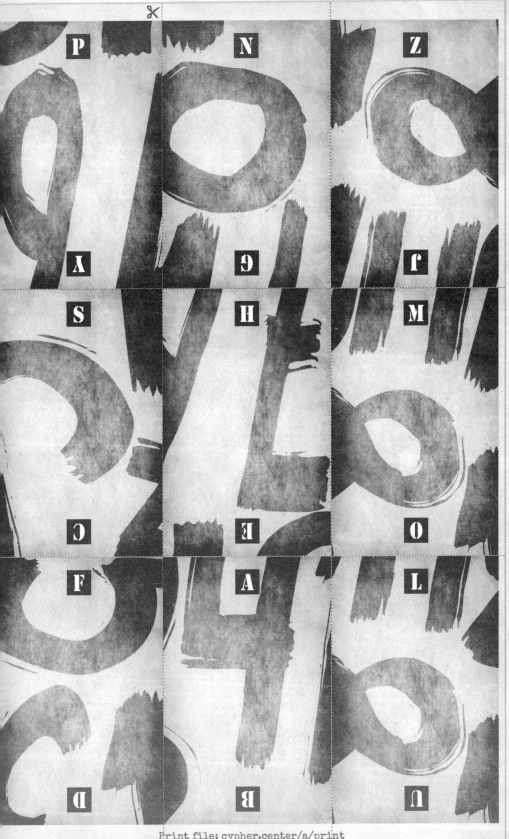

CREDITS

CREATED BY:
DIMITRIS CHASSAPAKIS

STORYLINE AND AGENT HANDLING BY:
STATHIS ATHANASIOU

VIKING

UK | USA | Canada | Ireland | Australia
India | New Zealand | South Africa

Viking is part of the Penguin Random House group of companies whose addresses
can be found at global.penguinrandomhouse.com.

First published 2020
001

Copyright © Dimitris Chassapakis, 2020

The moral right of the copyright holder has been asserted

Designed by Dimitris Chassapakis
Printed and bound in Great Britain by Clays Ltd, Elcograf S.p.A.

A CIP catalogue record for this book is available from the British Library

ISBN: 978-0-241-48174-5

www.greenpenguin.co.uk

MIX
Paper from
responsible sources
FSC® C018179

Penguin Random House is committed to a
sustainable future for our business, our readers
and our planet. This book is made from Forest
Stewardship Council® certified paper.